# ELIZABETH BEDLAM

# DEAD WHEN WE MET

COVER BY: **Elizabeth Bedlam**

FORMATTING BY: ELIZABETH BEDLAM

Published by: BEDLAM ! TYPEHOUSE / bedlam : typehouse

CREATED IN 2021 BY ELIZABETH BEDLAM

# READ THIS ★ DESTROY IT ☙ Burn it

CUT IT UP AND TAPE IT TO THE WALLS ...SOAK UP BLOOD ....USE TO BALANCE OUT A PIECE OF UNEVEN FURNITURE....

CONTACT ME OR DONT TO LET ME KNOW HOW IT GOES IF YOU SO DESIRE





BEDLAM TYPEHOUSE
MICHIGAN, USA
Instagram: @elizabeth.bedlam
Email: elizabethbedlam@gmail.com
Website: elizabethbedlam.com

Mona sat in the front window looking out over the dry brown lawn. The falling sun created long enticing shadows. They seemed to be reaching for her, wanting to wrap her in their dreamy embrace. *Fall into us, Mona.* Mona heard her grandmother shuffling down the back staircase that led into the kitchen.

*Later*, there would always be later.

Pulling the heavy curtains shut in the front room, she snapped on all four lamps(one in each corner). As she left the room she clicked on the ceiling fan, creating a starburst of pointed gloom(the only black in the room) among the fan blades. The bulbs were replaced with 100 watt warm white LED bulbs. They pushed any lingering drops of darkness from the room, leaving it stark with nowhere to hide.

Mona went to the dining room and pulled the six curtain panels across the wide picture window. Turned on the chandelier that held artificial candles. It was all the rage back then to decorate Georgian-style houses in faux colonial style. Electric candles, heavy dark woods against gaudy tartan wallpaper. Mona remembered Gran calling it *Bicentennial Chic*, or early Americana. Mona just called it ugly.

In the small television room she paused, picking at a corner of peeling wallpaper. She turned on the light as Gran came wandering in. She huffed and sat down heavy in a pea colored reclining chair. The fabric was nubby from ages of ass rubbing.

Up.

Down.

Side to Side.

Here.

There.

Gran had a beer in one hand, and was searching for the controller with the other. "Put my program on for me," she said.

Gran didn't know Mona's name these days, but she never forgot about her game shows. Mona could probably record one episode and play it every night and Gran would never be the wiser.

Mona pulled the chain on the floor lamp beside Gran. Fumbled around in the small magazine basket beneath it and pulled out the heavy square controller. Gran wouldn't buy a new television if she thought the old one worked perfectly fine. "We only get three channels Gran."

"That's all we need."

Mona didn't bother to argue. Gran would forget ten minutes later what they were talking about, and ask if Mona could make her a sandwich. Tomato smashed between two slices of brown bread, that's it. Mona couldn't sit at the table listening to Gran sucking that sopping wet mess into her mouth. She'd swipe her tongue along her lips, dragging in crumbs, yellow seeds suspended in bleeding goo of red nightshade.

It took a few moments for the television to warm up. When the picture came into focus Mona handed Gran the remote. "Another beer, Mallory," She'd say. Mona wasn't sure if Gran thought she was a nurse or some dead relative. These days Mona was more Mallory than Mona.

With Gran parked in front of her game show, the volume turned up as loud as the old thing would allow, Mona continued pulling blinds and curtains, switching on overhead lights. The house was too big. Five bedrooms, three and a half bathrooms. A study. Two living rooms. Huge kitchen with built in breakfast nook. Formal Dining room to the left. A front and back stairway. Nothing updated since 1978. It took an hour to close off all the windows and turn on every light. In the morning it took another hour to shut everything off and open all the drapes.

To save time Mona began buying a few timers each week to plug lamps into. No one was here anymore but her and Gran. Most of the family had moved out of state and had plenty of perfectly good excuses for never helping besides sending money. When Mona got out of the hospital a second time she had no way to support herself.

"Why don't you stay with Grandma? She's all alone in that big house. She'd love to have you." Aunt

Susan said.

Mona hadn't seen Gran in three years. She had no idea how bad her Alzheimer's had become. She'd never heard of sundowning until Aunt Susan explained what she'd have to do each night.

"There can be no shadows. Don't let her look outside. Trust me. This might seem like a pain in the ass, but it's much worse if you don't do it. Got it?"

Mona was only nineteen at the time. Now she was twenty-two and hadn't seen Aunt Susan in over a year. "How's she doing?" She'd ask over the phone. Susan got married and moved three states away only a month after Mona moved in.

These days it was just her and Gran. An endless rotating schedule of sleep and wake times. Medication. Meals. Dishes. Laundry. Bills. Groceries. Lights. The duties went on. Mona couldn't even look for a job because Gran couldn't be alone for more than a handful of minutes at a time. She only hoped she'd be able to stick it out and maybe get the house when Gran finally kicked the bucket in a few years.

She heard Gran slamming her fist on the little end table. "Mallory! I want my second beer!" She yelled. Her sharp, red knuckles pounding against the polished wood. It rattled the remote. Mallory came downstairs and heard the empty beer can being thrown across the room. It rattled falling to the ground, just missing a framed painting of a ship at sea.

Mona popped the top on another can. Gran refused to use a glass. "Mallory! And my Snickers!" She screamed again. Her voice was hoarse. It gave Mona the mental image of shredded pantyhose. The way they run and then pull apart forming large holes in the most awkward of places. She poured a cap full of nighttime cough syrup into the beer and swirled it around. It was the only way she could get out of the house at night.

That's what it took- two laced beers to put her down and keep her down until 6am. But until then, Mona dragged on.

Tonight was one of those nights. She felt the urge to get out and go see the man she read about in the paper. He was only thirty. His photo made him look so dignified. She read he'd been a teacher, so he probably loved children. He wasn't married. But even if he was, she didn't care. She didn't want to marry the guy, only fuck him.

Mona opened the cupboard over the sink. It was the only place Gran couldn't reach. She pulled out a Snickers bar from a box. She had enough stored for three months. It was all Gran would eat in the evening - 2 beers and a Snickers.

"About damn time, Mallory. I can't believe I'm paying you. Took so damn long now I gotta piss." Gran struggled to push herself out of the old chair. It groaned. Mona took her arm near the elbow to help her. "Get off. I'm not paying you extra to pretend to care. I can get up."

"You're not paying me, Gran." Mona said.

Gran eyed her. She got paranoid at night. You could set your watch by it. Sometimes Mona really questioned how much good it did trying to shut out the darkness. It felt as if it were already here, burrowed deep inside Gran, rearranging the book of memories within her mental library.

Maybe this darkness was inside herself as well. It made Mona feel better to think she wasn't really this way. It was something else inside her head, doing this to her. It wasn't her, it was Need... and she didn't put *Need* there. It simply was.

Need. Oh, Need. How could something she loved so much cause her so much mental anguish? *It wasn't natural.* That's what she read. But it felt natural to her. The open arms, the willingness to take her every time. Never any violence, or putting his needs before hers. He would never break her heart. He would never make her feel uncomfortable. He would never reject her as she grew older and faded.

Desire. The only thing that could strangle the barbed hook of Need. Some might say they are the same. Mona knew they were not. Need picked at her until she slashed her own wrists. It purred in wicked tones that she had no choice in the matter, but had do it anyway. She was a foul, unnatural creature for doing these things. But do them she must.  She hated Need.

But Desire. Desire was primal, almost Dionysiac in nature. Desire overcame Need the moment Mona saw him lying there, nude and washed, awaiting her touch. She would run just the tips of her fingers over fine cold bone wrapped in dry papery tissue. Inhaling sharply a biting tang of chemical death. He wouldn't move, just let her touch him, smell him. There was nothing else like it. Death was its own. One foot in this world, and one foot beyond. Nothing got Mona off like straddling that thin black line.

She tensed her thighs. Mona tried to pull Desire back in. It warmed her, made her deepest insides drip down out of her. It made her crave contact and forget about whether it was right or wrong. Need and Desire seemed to be working together tonight. She hadn't touched a body in months. The last one was right before she went into the hospital. She wanted to cut it out of her, and hope it would drain like a most ripe abscess. All the poison leaking out and drying on her bathroom floor.

Mona thought maybe that time it worked. She felt lightheaded, and couldn't remember what came afterward. It was over, she wouldn't be doing it again. The unrelenting torment of Need and Desire didn't matter, because she had moved beyond the cravings of the flesh to weightlessness of the spirit.

Or so she thought.

Then she woke up in the hospital, arms cleaned and covered. Her chest ached with sadness. She was still alive. Her mind went right back to that body.

Night surrounded the house, attempting to visit, but the lights turned it away. Gran was pacing in front of the television. She was telling the commercial why the game show host was wrong. What was he talking about? The show wasn't over, it had only just begun.

"Gran it's nine. Time to sleep." Mona didn't try to put gentle hands on Gran when she was pacing.

"Sleep? We only just got up. It's still light out!" She said, gesturing to the closed curtains.

"Gran? Why don't we go upstairs?"

And it went on like that for nearly two hours. Gran was ushered upstairs. The laced beer taking effect. She was agitated, but in the way a junkie was- slow, dazed. She would say she wasn't going to put on her nightgown as she slipped it down over her head. "Don't wash this everyday, you'll wear it out."

"I know, Gran."

"I like my stuff to smell like my stuff. Not some

fucking fuzzy bear."

"I know, Gran." Mona would help her into bed. Gran was getting heavy now. She laid back, closed her eyes. Muttered, but didn't demand. Mona turned the lights down only a notch, not enough to create threatening spills of shadows, but wading pools of charcoal. A gentle smudge on the wall or near a table. Never big enough to create a fright.

Mona went into her room and tossed on her black dress that hit her just above the knee. She slid her panties off. No one would notice. In the pocket of the dress she kept a small thin screwdriver, perfect for popping and twisting whatever locks stood between her and her man.

Mona slipped out the back door and walked three blocks to the cemetery. It was what she liked about Gran's house the most, how close it was to the dead. She didn't feel comfortable being gone for long periods of time. She couldn't take a bus an hour away.

Tombstones pushed out of the rolling hills of earth. It was easy to get lost in here. The trees stood still tonight, and faded into black. Mona felt a deep heavy peace walking among the dead. It wasn't a morbid feeling, like she wanted to be dead too. That need had passed in the hospital (for it seemed to rush in and out at will).

In moments like these it was more a reassuring calm, as if she wouldn't be alone forever. And until then the dead saw her as one of them in waiting. She was embraced by death, but not yet of it. Mona felt it all around her, a mossy softness cloaking her in comfort.

She liked that about death. So many things in life were uncertain. Mona didn't have any friends, she tried, but it never worked out. Inside she'd tell herself not to get excited when a living person talked to her, and she was always right. They always wanted something then disappeared until they were in need again.

Mona thought about Tim as she walked. Tim who she thought was a friend. He began talking to her, she didn't understand why. They were both in the hospital, he seemed friendly. It was only after she felt comfortably enough to talk to him that he suddenly pulled back. Then he'd only ask her questions like *what was the announcement they just said*, or *did she know what they were serving for lunch?* It never went any deeper.

The last time she saw Tim, she sat down and began telling him about a nightmare she had. He got up and walked away like she wasn't even there. Then he avoided her until she checked out a week later. It ached when she thought about it. Wondering what happened? Was she too friendly? But he seemed like he wanted to be friends. They had so much in common.

Then one day it was just over.

Mona tried to ignore her weird longing for a living connection. She had all she needed right in there. She stood before a white mausoleum. The door opened with only the protest of flaking rust grinding on iron hinges.

Inside was even more still. Nothing living existed within these walls except for Mona. She felt her vibrating life hitting against the solid unmoving forms of the building. As if by stepping inside time slowed down, but her body continued to age as rapidly as ever.

It would have been impossible to see but the stark white of the stone bled over any shadows, keeping them tucked in the corners, or drifting around the edges where they couldn't cause too much trouble. In front of her was a set of plain steel doors. She swallowed knowing where those doors led. On the other side a small family owned mortuary. She pressed against the doors and listened to the still silence. There was nothing living on the other side. She was sure. The man slumbered in eternity, waiting.

In her pocket she pulled out the newspaper square she had clipped from the obituary section. Nathan, everyone called him Nate. Killed in a motorcycle accident. Mona wondered how he would look. He seemed to be well liked. She bet his family was having any damage reconstructed. He would probably look even more perfect than his little black and white photograph.

Without too much trouble she used her screwdriver to turn over the lock on the door. It was a feeble attempt to keep people out. Or maybe they just didn't expect anyone would want to come in. The left side door opened silently into a dim room. An EXIT sign over the door emitted a hot red glow. Mona's very own red light district. Across the room she saw the white death shroud, beneath it her lover waited for her. He would never know her name, but she would remember his. She tried to remember them all. There had been four so far, Nate made five.

Her body pulled her forward. Moving among the shadows, no one would suspect anything living had entered the room. She made it her mission in life to be as silent as the dead she loved. She thought of herself as the living dead.

In the red cast she folded the sheet back. With eager fingers she touched him, cold and dry as old parchment. "Hello, there, sir." Her voice trembled. He was a beautiful solid man. She carefully brushed a few strands of his dark hair to the side.

Tomorrow he'd probably be dressed and prepared for his service. Tonight he was free from all that. Death's decorations she called it. The flowers and fancy clothes. The perfumes and corpse paint. How she hated that corpse paint. Here he was washed out and raw. Remains of a man for her to gather and take into herself.

"No, need for penetration." She told him on this warm evening. She was glad to do all the work. "You just lay back and enjoy yourself." Mona kissed his thick lips. He tasted preserved. Sterile and chemical with a hint of frosted human musk.

Mona climbed onto the table. Her back to his face. She crawled backward until her sex was over his face. She loved the feeling when she lowered herself down. The chill of the corpse's mouth on her aroused cunt.

She admired his flaccid cock, a respectable size. Maybe in life he was a decent lover. She'd never know. She didn't really care. She did know tonight she would make him into a great lover. She began to move back and forth, putting her weight on him, bending forward and putting his cock in her mouth.

The hot salty taste of a man was gone, and replaced with a barren cold. As she warmed up she dropped the cock from her mouth to gasp at the heat spreading from between her legs to her thighs. She was moving quicker now. She brought her pelvis down hard on the dead man's mouth.

Her weight on his chest pushed fluids up out of his loosely stitched mouth making a wet mess. Actual sex with the dead (man or woman) was rarely a clean act. This was one thing that didn't differ from living sex. Any good sex was filthy, wet, and completely encompassing when you got right down to it. When you let go of your inner stream of thoughts, closed your eyes and just felt your body mounting towards those few moments of nothing but pure all encompassing humanity. It pushed you past your common everyday self and into another state of consciousness all together. You couldn't stop even if you wanted.

If someone appeared before Mona during this time she would have no choice but to lock eyes with them and continue riding the face of Nathan, letting them watch her. And she would like it- them watching her orgasming into the mouth of this beautiful dead body. That made her hotter. It burnt her through like a grease fire over water.

She wanted to scream, feeling her conscience being rushing from her head to her cunt, mounting until it blossomed outwards. She tensed, pushed herself up and arched her back. She was grinding down onto his face until her passion lashed out in a final hot spark and she gasped.

Mona exhaled and fell forward, her face landing on his soft thick cock. She nuzzled it, tightening her thighs, taking in the last burning embers of her climax. She dragged herself across his face lightly a few more

times, getting it all out, until she finally felt drained.
She had been away too long. This was natural to her.
She was honoring the human form with her Need and
Desire.

Her cunt was soaking wet when she finally
rolled herself off. She throbbed for more, but knew better than to linger. It was getting late. "Good night, Nathan." She stood a moment, admiring him. The smear
of whatever bubbled from his lips lashed across his
face. She kissed the air, *mwah*! and threw up the sheet.
It fell lightly over his form. Once a man, then a lover,
now a ghost.

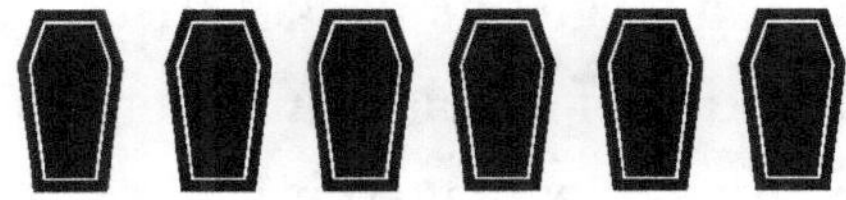

On her walk back home, Mona enjoyed the
sticky feeling between her legs. The juices, a remind-
er of what she had just done. It thrilled her and turned
her on like no pulsing man could. She'd tried. She was
still trying. She always thought if she could just find the
*right* guy, maybe this picking urge would cease.

From everything she read, sex with the dead
wasn't what a well adjusted person did. Especially not
a woman. Nine out of ten necrophiliacs were men she
heard. This made her feel more alien than ever. A girl
in a boys club. She chatted with a handful of necros
from across the world. All men. She promised them her

body if she died young.

She'd try to kill herself twice. Once after her first time with a corpse. The shame overwhelmed her. A second time when a boyfriend broke up with her. She felt she could tell him anything, but she was wrong. Fucking corpses was one thing he would not accept. She didn't say she had actually done it, only that it was a fantasy. She thought about it. "You're a fucking freak, Mona. Jesus Christ! Do you hear yourself?!" He screamed at her while she cried she was sorry. She was joking. *Please don't leave...*

Gran didn't know it, but in her room downstairs Mona kept a large oak casket. It had deep scratch marks from decades of display. A funeral home was going to trash it, but she salvaged it and paid to have it delivered. The velvet interior was worn in spots. On the inside of the lid she had pinned cut out photos of cadavers and newspaper obituary photos of her lovers. A few had hearts drawn around them, or the date of their love affair.

In the dark of her oak box sometimes her tears would overwhelm her. The loneliness she felt deep within herself. A hole that rotted in the center of her chest, that ached whenever she thought about how hard it was just being alive. Millions of people and it was just her. In this house.

When she wasn't thinking about being wrapped

around a dead man, she thought about her own suicide plans. She went back and forth, wondering if she
should try for the third time. Some days were better
than others. Tonight suicide felt far away. Tomorrow at
this time, she couldn't be sure.

She felt no one would notice, not even Gran. She
kept on wishfully thinking maybe things would get better. Necrophiliacs she talked to online were support-
ive. But they were little icons spread across the plan-
et. They didn't feel real. Would they even notice if
she dropped off the board? Or just go on as usual. As
she told herself, today wasn't so bad. But who knows
what she would feel like tomorrow. Sometimes the not
knowing, the up and downs, were worse than anything.
To feel so happy, but know you wouldn't stay like that
no matter how hard you clung on, was enough to drive
someone crazy.

Her neighbor, Charles, was standing in his front
yard next to the sidewalk. A lemon pool of streetlamp
light encircling him. He was a few years younger than
her. He was draped in his heavy red cloak, and looking
grim. "Where you come from?" He asked.

"Just out for a walk."

Charles nodded, his hood sliding back. He

reached to pull it over his eyes. Regaining his serious face. "Waiting for your ride?" She asked, standing in front of him.

"Yeah. Assholes are always late." He shook his head. Mona didn't know why he wore that cloak. It was either for a game or a cult. She never found a comfortable way of asking him. Maybe he just liked to wear it and it had nothing to do with anything. Maybe he enjoyed wearing it, just as she enjoyed fucking corpses. A comfort level of sorts. You can't explain it to anyone, but it's real so it must be true.

"Well, see ya, Charles."

"Have a good night, Mallory."

"Mona." She said, turning to look at him.

"Huh?"

"I'm not Mallory. I'm Mona."

"Really? Hm." A car pulled up and he nodded and went to climb in. Mona watched the group drive off. Charles was the only one in a red cloak. The rest looked harmless enough. Had he really thought her name was Mallory? Or was he messing with her? Mona shook her head, she could never tell with that guy.

Charles was more interesting than anyone she met in the hospital. He did a lot of drugs a few years back and was now convinced he was receiving messages though the tin foil. He'd talked about maybe eating a few of the pieces to see if he could interpret what they said. "I think it's some sort of high frequency. Like only brain waves can pick it up," He went on one afternoon when he and Mona were sitting out back smoking cigarettes.

"Won't that hurt your teeth?" She asked.

"It would be worth it, don't you think? What if it's telling me the secret of life? Or that the FBI is watching me. Aliens know this shit, they could be trying to warn me. Or maybe they want me to help save humanity from a global meltdown? I wouldn't know because I'd be too chicken shit scared of hurting my teeth. I'm going to try it." He said.

"No, Charles, don't. There's no messages." Mona told him. He shrugged and sat back in the lawn chair, seeming to forget about it. They watched the sprinkler click back and forth across the parched grass.

Mona slipped into the house. The brightness of the lights made her squint until her eyes adjusted. She listened and heard nothing, thankful Gran was still asleep. She always felt guilty when she came back. She was out having a good old time while Gran was at home drugged out her head, growing more confused by the day.

As she headed into her room she told herself what she told herself every time, *don't feel guilty*. She spent all day everyday caring for Gran and running her life. It was perfectly fine that she had a few hours to herself in the evening to go out. It wasn't like she was drinking or fucking men she met at a bar. She was just going for an evening walk, a little stress release. If she didn't, she feared she'd develop an ulcer, or go just as crazy as Gran. What would two deranged women do in this house? Probably set it on fire and then laugh while it burned down around them, forgetting they too were inside.

Mona went into the bathroom and ran cool water into the discolored pink bathtub. Lowering herself down into the pool she felt the stiff residue of sex on her inner thighs begin to lift. She released a heavy sigh and sank lower, thinking about her corpse lover. She couldn't imagine being attracted to him as a living breathing man. He probably drank too much beer and watched football, ignoring his girlfriend. Obituaries always made saints out of the dead. She wondered what hers would say.

*Mona Weatherwax, 22, died alone on October 2, at her Grandmother's home.*

*As was her request, no memorial or service will be held.*

*Ms. Weatherwax was born here, died here. She was a filthy sinning corpse-fucker.*

*It's no wonder she took her own life. No one would ever love her. She never had a*

*A real job. She barely graduated high school. May she burn in Hell for all time.*

Yeah, that sounded about right. Mona felt around for a washcloth to scour the insides of her thighs. When she was finished she was red and smelled like Jasmine. Another sin washed away. She wondered if anyone would notice the molested state of the corpse in the morning. Probably not. He was dead. They'd just dress him up and roll him out. Hopefully they'd clean his mouth up a bit.

Mona pulled on a t-shirt and panties, walked through to her room. She never bought a bed, but slept in her salvaged casket. She set the alarm on her clock. The little metal hammer would smash against two bells until she awoke. It was the only thing loud enough to wake her before Gran. Even inside the box she could hear the *click-click-click* near her ear. Besides that it was like sleeping inside a shell.

So silent, just the clicking of the clock growing more distant as she drifted off. Her ears heard the soft static of the universe swirling around her. Her breathing echoing off the interior sides of the casket. In the dark she looked up at the lid, and felt she was falling backwards away from those cut out pictures of corpses.

Or maybe she wasn't falling, but speeding up and going forward, her body in a rapid state of decay. She was running into death's arms. The ultimate endless love. Chilled skin, empty staring eyes, sometimes sew shut as if she was fucking him in his sleep. Rubbing her clit against a solid, uncaring empty husk. Sometimes a body would have the most exquisite bruising. Shades of deep purple to black where blood had pooled for sometime. The rest of the body empty of flush, pale as the white horse on which death rides.

The metallic banging on the other side of the casket woke Mona with a start. She sat upwards, hit her head. She was awake. Mona pulled her clothes on and looked at herself in the mirror. Examined her eyes, they were bloodshot. Picked at her teeth, they were stained. It's a good thing she wanted the dead, because she couldn't think of a living man who would want her. At least not this early in the morning.

But Gran didn't care what she looked like so Mona got on with it. Making Gran the exact same thing every morning. Two eggs, black Columbian coffee. Gran never forgot these things either. Mona couldn't get away with making cereal or cutting up fruit.

Gran and her ate in silence. Gran read the newspaper every morning. She complain about politics every morning. "Damn fascists pigs" she'd mutter. "If your father could see this he'd roll over in his damn grave!" She'd bash her fist on the table. Mona ignored it when Gran referred to her as a daughter or a nurse or anything else other than Mona. She was pretty sure Gran didn't even know Mona existed.

"Why don't we take you into the front room, then I'll clean up." Mona walked beside Gran not touching her. In the front room she threw open the curtains to let in the hazy sun. By noon this room would feel like a furnace and she'd have to close them again. Gran fiddled with her basket, pulled out a skein of yarn and proceeded to work on a gray scarf that was longer than any scarf had business being.

Mona pulled up the shade over the sink. While washing dishes she looked out into the backyard. She could see Charles passed out in a lawn chair. A deep red velvet pile. His ashy hair stark against the faded tones of late summer. He was so still, she wondered if he was dead. Knew he was probably just hung over.

Looking over her shoulder, she heard the clicking of Gran's needles. Mona dried her hands on her pants and walked out the back door across her lawn to his. "Hey," she said, poking him.

Charles didn't move. Mona reached over and went through his cloak searching for his pack of smokes. Gran somehow always knew when Mona was hiding cigarettes in the house. She'd find them and smoke the whole pack. One right after another. It was worse than her Snickers bar habit.

Mona flicked over the top of the narrow steel lighter, lit her cigarette, snapped it shut, then threw it at Charles who was just starting to come around. "Why are you sleeping out here?" She asked. Charles opened one eye and looked at her, pushed himself up from his slouched corpse pose.

"Mom locked the door. Or...it was jammed. Either way I couldn't get it open."

"I thought you didn't do drugs anymore, Charles."

"Huh? No, I don't. Why would you say something like that?"

"The door wouldn't open so you slept in that shitty lawn chair? You were probably high as a kite, man." Mona laughed, exhaled soft smoke into the morning. It was already humid. She hoped it would rain soon. It didn't rain enough anymore. No, Mona decided that was wrong. It didn't *storm* enough anymore. Thunderstorms, winds, pounding rain. Whatever happened to those storms? Mona couldn't remember the last time she feared for her life during a flash of lightning.

"Why are you hassling me, Mal?"

"Mona."

"Whatever. You're smoking my cigarette, sitting in my lawn chair. Go open the door. Go ahead." He said.

"You're serious?"

"Go try to open the damn door," he told her again.

Mona sighed, standing up. She walked up to his back door, looked over her shoulder at him. "Go on," he told her.

Mona tried the knob, it turned in her hand, but the door didn't open. It felt loose, not locked, but as if missing a screw. She pushed in with all her weight, trying to twist. The door remained unmoved by her efforts.

"What about the front door?" She asked.

He shrugged. "Didn't try it."

Mona heard Gran yelling something from inside. She sighed and crushed her cigarette into the grass. "I'll see you later." She said, getting up to leave.

"Hey, you want to go out sometime?" Charles asked.

"No."

"Whatever..." she heard Charles mutter, knowing he was as unmoved as her. Mona still couldn't figure out what his deal was. If he was crazy, a recovering addict, or just eccentric. She liked the guy, even if he never did go anywhere without that velvet cloak. But the possibility of rolling around in the sheets with him made her as dry as sand. He'd be grabbing at her, twisting her tits around.

He probably liked role playing and would make her say all kinds of stupid things. Then she thought, *what if he did like role playing?* Would he role play for her? Would he play corpse for her? If she could just find a way of channeling her lust for death into a living man, maybe she could change. She could be almost normal, and just have a little fetish like a normal girl. Hm...

Mona stopped by the back door, letting the possibility roll through her brain. Would it hurt to try? Gran was ranting inside, something about how the angels had finally come to claim her. Mona turned back to Charles who was still sprawled out in the chair. He always wore black jeans under that robe. She wondered how many pairs he had. How many robes did he have?

"Charles!" She yelled.

He rolled his head over in her direction, "Huh?"

"I think I will go out with you. Tonight?"

"Cool."

"I'll come over after Gran is asleep."

"Uh-huh. See ya." He waved, his voice the same tone, slightly bored and suspicious.

Mona pushed inside, the cool air of the house made her nipple poke out from under her tank top. She would bother to put on a bra if she had bigger tits, but she really, in all honesty, didn't see the point. If a man could be fifty pounds overweight, with bigger breasts than hers, and go out to mow the grass, she shouldn't have to subject herself to hooks and straps in ninety degree temperatures.

"Gran, what is it?" Mona followed the shouts and found Gran circling her casket in the middle of the bedroom. "Gran, what are you doing in here?" She gently took her grandmother's arm and attempted to lead her away.

"No, Mallory. This is for me. Don't you see? The angels, they must know....oh...Death has come to our house." Gran crossed herself. "I'm supposed to sleep here and wait my turn. Here help me in." Gran lifted up the top half with moderate difficulty, attempted to lift the second half but failed. "Mallory!" She shouted to a stunned granddaughter.

"Gran this isn't for you. It's mine. Gran, please don't sleep in there. Gran!" Mona watched as Gran pushed up the bottom door and began to climb in.

"No, this is perfect." Gran settled down and looked up at Mona. Mona had no idea how she'd get Gran out of her box. "This isn't so bad. Kinda comfy." She wiggled her old sack of bones about.

"Gran, you can't sleep in there. Come on, let me help you out." Mona reached for her.

"Damn it, Mallory. No! This is my bed. I will be buried in it. It's Death's will! Why else would it be here? If this is what he wants, then fine. I am ready. Take me Death!" She sang, her hands shaking with devotion. Mona stood there chewing her lip.

She really didn't know what else to do. Gran was not climbing out. Mona couldn't lift her out. She thought about getting Charles to see if he could pick her up, but figured it was a waste of time. Charles probably never lifted anything heavier than a bag of chips in his life. "Fine, Gran. That's where you want to sleep then?"

Mona reached over and pulled down the corpse photos. Gran was nodding her head. "Bring me my basket. I might as well finish that scarf while I wait." Gran pushed herself into a sitting position, her legs stretched out in the casket.

Mona did as she was told, bringing Gran her knitting basket. "And a beer, ice cold." Gran told her.

"It's only ten in the morning. Don't you think it's a little early?"

"I'm dying! Who gives a damn?!" Gran snapped and began fiddling with her yarn. Mona wasn't in the mood. She couldn't believe she lost her casket to Gran, who apparently not only wanted to sleep in it, but live in it, awaiting her death. Then as a last stab in Mona's chest, be buried with the thing. Mona got Gran's beer and resisted throwing it at her.

"Now leave. I want to be alone for reflection." Gran took a loud sip from the can and began knitting. Mona stood there a second and threw up her hands. It looked like her casket banging role playing with Charles would have to change locations. Would it be too much to hope that he had a coffin?

"That's cool." Charles said that evening when Mona told him about her fantasy. "I can play dead."

"Really? You wouldn't happen to have a coffin would you?"

"Nah. But they never lock the mausoleums down the road. You can fuck me there if you want. I'm not picky."

"How do you know they never lock them?"

Charles shrugged, "I go in there sometimes to look for bones and stuff."

The two began walking towards the cemetery. This was a whole other side to Charles Mona knew nothing about. "Bones for what?"

"Just collecting... Selling... Whatever..." He looked at her from under his hood.

"Aren't you hot in that thing? Why do you always wear it anyway?"

"Why do you want to fuck a dead guy?"

The two walked on in silence. A sign said the grounds were closed after dark, but the gate was wide open. Mona followed Charles, acting as if she didn't know the place better than the back of her own hand. He walked past the one she usually went to and continued to a dilapidated one in the back. The glass was broken out of the iron door. Leaves of rust pulled off when Charles swung it open. The whole scene made Mona feel a little sad.

"In there?" She asked.

"You got a better place?" He stood just inside the door. It truly did look like death was awaiting her, his hood draped over his face. Strokes of shadows helped blur out his humanity. Mona felt she really had to try. How nice would it be to have an understanding boyfriend? Maybe she could get into this.

"No, it's fine," she said, stepping up into the gloom. The place had no windows, and the inside was covered with graffiti. "I hate shit like that." Mona made a mental note to come back during the day to scrub off the stupid *dead inside* red letters carelessly scrawled across the four drawers that were inside. "People are such assholes."

Charles snuffed, "You're figuring that out now?"

"No. Just reaffirming my beliefs." She told him, not squinting too hard to see him in the dark.

"So you want me to lie on the floor? Or I can just fuck you against the wall." Charles said pulling his pants off, but leaving his robe in place.

"Um, no, just lie down. Are you sure no one will come back here?" Mona thought about closing the door, but realized with the broken glass it wouldn't do much good.

"I'm here all the time. I never see anyone but you," Charles said. His comment caught her off guard.

"What do you mean?"

"Come on, Mona. You know. Why do you think I wasn't surprised you wanted to come here?" He laid down on the ground, pulled up the red velvet to reveal his erection. It was that easy. Mona exhaled sharply and looked down at his cock.

She was here in her black dress without panties. He was here with his pants off and a hard on. She couldn't waste this opportunity.

Gran was at home passed out in the casket. She only had so much time, worried Gran might awaken and forget she had chosen to sleep in the box of her own free will. Mona would feel horrible if Gran died of fright because she wasn't there to soothe her.

"Don't talk, okay?" She said hiking up her dress and squatting over him, her back turned to his face.

"So you want me to just lie here? I can't touch you?"

"What did I just say? No talking. Just be still. Pretend you're dead or this isn't going to work," she snapped.

Charles didn't say anything. He struggled to remain silent and still as Mona pushed down on him, taking him into her wet cunt. He wanted to grab her hips and tell her to fuck him into the ground. He liked the pain of the cold stone floor. He'd like it better if she would cut him and tear his nipple off with her teeth. But he didn't say any of that. Instead he closed his eyes and tried to hold still while she arranged him inside her moist, warm interior.

Mona closed her eyes and thought about the dead men she'd fucked, their smell, their tight skin, their limp sex. She pretended Charles had rigor mortis of the cock, that's why he was so stiff. She should treasure this. She hadn't been penetrated since her last living boyfriend. She sighed, moving up and down, riding him, grinding him down.

Instead of the smell of a fresh corpse, she inhaled scents of candle wax and dried leaves from the small altar against the far wall. "Fuck Charles, this isn't working." She gasped after a few minutes.

"What about some bones?"

"Huh?"

"Here, get up." Charles told her. Mona stood and Charles pushed himself to his feet, his erection begging for more. With needy hands he pulled open the far drawer. Mona shouldn't be surprised it had been prided open and vandalized already. Charles glanced over at her in the dark. "Don't look at me like that, I didn't pry it open."

He rummaged through the drawer. "Want a skull or an arm?"

"Hm. Skull I guess," Mona said. Charles handed her a smooth skull the color of a tea stain. Charles laid back on the floor, exposing his urgent need. If she didn't do something about it soon he was going to jerk off in that skull's gaping eye socket.

Mona shoved him back in. The heat from his cock made it hard to fantasize he was dead. She pushed the skull down to her cunt, and rubbed her clit across it's beautifully blemished surface. She rubbed the dry bone back and forth as she rode Charles' living one. *God, sweet mortality.* Someday she would be as this skull is now.

Mona felt her own living desire building as she pushed herself up and down on Charles, her knees biting into the unforgiving ground. Her muscles were tense and began to ache. She was fucking Charles, but the skull was fucking her. She rolled her head back and felt herself riding an orgasmic thread that wove together lust and death. It was everything she needed. She opened her eyes as she finished, taking in the grim bleakness of the tomb. Outside the door she saw the rows of soft crumbling headstones in the night.

Her final gasp, her orgasm's death rattle, drained her, she crumbled forward, her head resting a second near Charles's knees. The skull still shoved tightly against her gash. "Fuck, Mona..." Charles exhaled.

His words made Mona cringe and remember his cock. It was falling out of her, useless and limp, and still warm. His hands were lightly massaging the back of her thighs. "You've got a really nice ass, you know that?"

Mona continued to grip onto the skull. She turned and looked back at Charles, "Do you think it's cool if I take this?" She asked him.

"I guess, I've already got three," he said. Mona stood up, feeling his seed run down the interior of her leg. She was used to her own mucus and chilled corpse fluid. This feeling of warm glue made her shudder. She couldn't wait to get home and scrub her cunt out.

"Fuck, my back." Charles got up, deciding the pain from the stone floor wasn't the kind of pain he had in mind. "Next time, why don't we do it in the grass? Or bring a blanket or something? I'm going to have a fucking bruise now."

Mona wasn't listening but admiring the glistening skull in the darkness. "Would you do that?" Charles asked. "Mona?" His hand on her waist made her feel stiff. She didn't like to be touched afterwards. The grabbing hands, like she wasn't free to go when she wanted. He opened his mouth like he wanted to say something, but stuttered before falling silent.

"*What*?" She shrugged him off and walked outside to inhale the wet summer night that clung to the hot stones.

"Cut me," he said, following her. She turned and looked at him. His face again was obscured by his hood.

"Cut you?"

"Not deep, just like across the chest...or maybe..."

"What, Charles? Just say it," she sighed. "I just fucked a skull while riding your cock in a graveyard. What?"

"Nothing, just abuse of any kind. Cutting or punching... Kicking in the balls... Anything," he swallowed.

Mona sighed. She would be more than happy to kick him in the balls. "That's fine, Charles. If there is a next time."

Charles regained his uncaring, apathetic tone. "Yeah, of course. I've got plenty of chicks that I'm fucking, so it's just whatever."

"Uh-huh. Can we go?" Mona asked, realizing

she'd left Gran longer than she meant to. Neither talked on the way home. Mona had Charles carry the skull under his cloak until they were at the back door.

Charles handed her the bone. In the dim light it could be nothing more than a large stone. "Do you know his name?" Mona asked, turning the relic around in her hands, running a thumb over the smooth, empty socket that once held eyes. Eyes that took in the world around him. These sights absorbed through the delicate pink nerves up into his brain, filled this skull with memories.

Mona was shocked by how much emotion was filling her. Running from the cold cranium into her hands, as if she were absorbing some part of him into herself. She'd never brought remains home with her.

"I think it was Frank Something," Charles said.

"Frank... Hello, Frank." Mona said in the darkness, her voice breathy. Almost forgetting Charles was there. She didn't feel like she had fucked him. But that it was her and Frank, Charles just happened to be there too. She petted the skull in the dark, Charles shifted from one foot to the other.

"So I'll call you?" he said, leaning down to kiss her. Mona turned away.

"I see you everyday," She said. "Night. Thanks for this." She opened the door and went inside. Shut it. Didn't look back. The lock turned over. Charles stood

in the dark a moment longer, trying to decide if that
went well or not. He got laid. Mona didn't slap him.
She liked her skull gift. Yes, he decided. It went better
than he thought it would.

His cloak dragged on the grass as he sauntered
over the lawn to his house. The back door was still
jammed. He didn't bother walking around. Instead he
sat down in the lawn chair, stared up at Mona's house.
All the windows were covered. He wondered if she was
going to masturbate with the skull. He hated that he
wanted to watch.

Mona had almost forgotten Gran was asleep
in her casket. She couldn't even go use her bathroom.
She sighed. There were four other bedrooms to choose
from. She chose the other on the first floor, just in case
Gran woke up in a fright. She didn't want her box or
gran any more damaged than they already were.

She set Frank beside the sink in the tiny lavender bathroom. This was considered to be a guest bed/
bath so everything was half the size. There was no bub-
ble bath. Mona would have to just deal with it for a
night. If gran insisted on moving in her room she'd
move her soap and toothbrush out tomorrow. She
didn't even really miss her corpse photos though, she

had Frank.

His empty black sockets observed silently as she undressed for him. He had already been smashed into her gash, so it wasn't like he hadn't seen it all before. But something about him watching her, Mona liked it. She liked it a lot. She hardly ever got time alone with a corpse, or in this case, a piece of it.

Mona turned on the water, filling the tub. She began to slowly unbutton her little black dress. Frank sat, unmoving, watching her strip before him in the cramped lavender tiled bath. There was no point in playing coy, she let the frock fall to the ground and she stepped out, only in her bra. "More?" She asked.

Frank said nothing, just how she liked it. Her foot broke the surface of the cool water. Frank watched her, a grin that told her he liked what he was seeing. Mona climbed in returning his stare. Though better of it and got half way up and snatched Frank from the sink edge, brought him down into the water with her.

"You're filthy. If we're going to keep sleeping together I think you need a good scrub." Forgetting about herself Mona, with the tender hands of a lover, wiped Frank down with a soft green washcloth. She removed the soiled grime and the crust of her sex from the frontal lobe. Wiped him until he glistened, a few sepia blotches here and there. She wondered how old he was. Fifty or eighty years? The tomb looked like no one had been buried in it in decades.

Mona laid back and lifted Frank up close to her face. She wiped a trickle of water that ran from his eye socket. "You might be the only one who understands me, Frank." She said, continue to caress him, run her fingers over the edges where his nose would have sprouted.

Holding him so close to her Mona brought him to her and pressed her lips to his. A real first kiss. Her tongue lingered over his teeth, rounded but firm. So smooth, like she was licking cold glass. She cracked his jaw just enough to slip her tongue into the empty space beyond. She hadn't really kissed anyone like this for a while. Maybe ever. Mona's heart picked up it's face and she and Frank got to know each other. As her tongue explored the roof of his mouth.

She'd already fucked Charles, but that didn't feel real. Mona didn't feel anything, but desire for Frank. She leaned back in the tub and closed her eyes, picturing all of him, draped over her like a stitched quilt of bones. "Frank..." she muttered, slipping the skull between her legs, pressing his hard, polished surface to her soft, warm one.

Mona's gasp was heavy and rolled out of her, as if someone dropped a rug and the dust came rolling out in a curled wave. It sent ripples across the scummy surface of the bathwater. She moved Frank quicker back and forth between her legs, pressing as hard as before, only this time Charles wasn't there to warm her. The cooling water, her and Frank were alone.

Her legs pressed into either cover of the tub, and she held Frank tight against her, masturbating herself with death. She was a quiet lover, only moaning, and gasping in the back of her throat. The top of her head resting on the little square tiles behind her. Her stomach tightened, and her arms were beginning to ache from the force of her almost desperate act. She wanted Frank to get her off so bad, she knew he could be enough.

*"Oh, ah... oh... Frank..."* and she inhaled sharply creating a high pitch among the splashes of the bath. They were her words as she finally climbed down the other side of orgasm. Her legs trembled afterwards, her body filling with the hum of being alive, but the skull of a dead man was still between her legs. A place where life was to be embraced, born from. Death was not to be shoved up there, into a cradle of life. But Mona tried, and that got off more than Charles' throbbing cock and thigh massages did.

She set Frank to the side of the tub and just soaked a moment longer, taking in air and relaxing. It had been a better night than she thought it would be. She went out with a living man, and came home with the head of a dead one. If only she had her casket's warm velvet to crawl back into. Instead she'd have to settle for old white bed linens printed with tiny yellow daisies.

Mona laid down, Frank on the bedside table. The empty cool air above her. Frank on the table, over there. It didn't feel right to her. She wanted them to be cuddled close in warm darkness. She tossed and turned, looking at the little travel clock. It's white hands had neon green strips that glowed in the dark. She was going to be exhausted tomorrow if she didn't get some sleep.

"Come on, Frank." Mona dropped out of bed onto the ground, grabbed Frank and crawled under the bed frame. Mona reached outwards and felt the steel rails running horizontal. They were cold and hard, only mere inches from her face. "Good night, Frank." She whispered.

She turned on her head to the side and gently nuzzled the side of his gently protruding cheek bone. This felt better. She cradled Frank more as if he were a teddy bear in her arms than a dusty old skull her date had pilfered from a desecrated crypt. Tomorrow the nurse was coming to do checks on Gran. That would take about two hours. Instead of going to the grocery store, like usual, Mona decided to slip off and tidy up Frank's family's crypt.

The alarm pinged. Mona groaned. She felt for Frank, he had rolled off in the night. She turned her head and saw him sitting cock-eyed just out of reach. "Morning" She crawled out from under the bed and plucked him up from the carpet.

Mona liked this part, she kissed him good morning. She had morning breath, but it didn't matter to him. "You have to stay here while Gran is awake. You understand. She doesn't need any more reminders of death."

She perched Frank on the edge of the toilet tank while she got dressed and brushed her teeth. "I'm going to clean up your family's crypt today. I'll try and scrub that fucking graffiti off. Just straighten up a bit." She told him. His empty sockets approved of her, both in actions and looks. She turned to him, "I really like having you here, Frank." She kissed Frank again and set him in the cabinet under the sink next to the bleach. "See you later." She waved and closed the doors, leaving Frank grinning in the dark.

Mona rushed around opening windows and switching off lights. She was boiling coffee when Gran emerged. "How'd you sleep?"

"I think I want the lid closed." Gran said, sitting down slow and steady in the steel chair. The vinyl seat cracked and Gran arranged herself.

"It's too dark. It needs to stay open. That's the deal. Maybe you should go back to your bed. It's probably more comfortable." Mona suggested setting breakfast in front of Gran. But Gran refused.

"That is my bed now. Death's bed." She said, her eyes popping just a little.

"You're being over dramatic Gran. You've got lots of time left." Mona said, sitting down across from her. To this Gran laughed, quietly at first, then louder until she filled the house.

"You must think I'm real stupid, Mallory." She said after a minute. The knocking at the back door topped Mona from answering. Mona looked at Gran who got up and wandered away. She never talked to anyone who came to the door. She always made Mona do it. Even if the person asked repeatedly for the homeowner, Gran still refused to talk to them.

Mona pushed her hair out of her face and felt it was going to be a long day. Another knock. She snapped up the shade and saw Charles standing on the other side. He jumped then waved silent through the window. Mona groaned, she didn't feel like talking to him this morning. She already knew what he wanted, but opened the door anyway.

"Hey," she said.

"Hey," he said.

Both stood in silence. "So do you want something?" Mona asked. She had to gather up some cleaning supplies, locate a scrub brush. The nurse would be here soon.

Charles furrowed his brow, looked unsure if he should say what he was thinking. "Just thinking about last night," he finally said.

"Oh, yeah? What about it?"

This caught him off guard, like he expected her to say something else like *me too*. Now he'd have to scramble for a new line. "Just, uh, it was fun. I liked it."

"Uh-huh. Great."

"Want to go out again tonight?" He was aching for her. He'd play dead for her. She was the strangest woman he'd ever met, and he couldn't get her out of his head.

"No."

That remark also caught him off guard. He thought the sex was good. She got off. Didn't she enjoy herself? Plus he let her keep Frank. "No, huh? What about tomorrow?"

"Probably not. It just wasn't what I wanted, Charles. It wasn't you. It's not your fault you're not, um...you know."

"We could try again. If you want a coffin I could probably get one. What do you think about that?"

This gave Mona pause. What did she think

about that? She couldn't afford a new casket. No he would still be too hot for her. Plus now she had Frank. She thought briefly about last night in the bathtub. That space right between the eyebrows, it was smooth and shiny. Her rubbing vigorously against her clit. The seeping of lust out of her body, instead of some guy blowing it into hers.

"Charles, I don't think so." He opened his mouth to counter her, but she stopped him. "Look, I've got a lot to do today. Gran's nurse is coming by and I've got some errands to run. I've really got to go. We'll talk later, okay?" She slammed the door before he could say another word.

Charles walked back across the lawn, sat in the lawn chair. Pulled out a small bit of tin foil and looked at it. He looked back at Mona's house. He knew he shouldn't have given her that fucking skull. She probably fucked it all last night, and again this morning. It wasn't his fault he wasn't dead. He sighed, looked back down at the creased tin foil square. How up and wandered around the side of the house to his front door. The bottom of his cloak was wet from the morning dew.

Gran saw him pass by the window of the sitting room. "Mallory! Mallory! He's here, he's come for me!" Gran shouted, throwing her knitting needles aside. The sudden outburst made Mona jump and smack her head under the kitchen sink. She ran into the other room, scrub brush still clutched in her hand.

"Gran what is it? Who? What happened?" Mona looked at the mess of tangled yarn, Gran peering out the window into the side yard.

"Death, I saw him. He just passed by. Oh, the crows are circling, Mallory."

"What are you talking about?" Mona went to the window and stood beside Gran. She saw a crimson flash of a cape disappear around the corner of a neighbor's house. "Gran, that's not death." Mona exhaled. "It's just Charles. He lives next door with his mother. Remember? He wears that cape. I don't know why. Gran calm down."

Gran was breathing heavily. Her head bobbing back and forth trying to get a closer look. The doorbell rang. Gran yelped in the back of her throat. "It's Him." She gasped.

"What? No Gran it's probably just the nurse. Gran?" Mona's grandmother was clutching at her left shoulder, uttering to herself. Mona yelled for the nurse to come on. She helped Gran lay down on the sofa. The nurse heard the yells and came rushing in to help.

During the funeral Mona realized she had forgotten all about cleaning up Frank's family's crip. That was three days ago. From where she stood, she could see the sharp peak of the roof among the trees. Mona shifted her foot from side to side, eager to be done with it. She was tired of getting hugged by strangers.

She didn't care if she shared blood with them, she didn't know them. They didn't know her. Only what her mother had told them, so probably lies. Mona hadn't spoked to her mother in over a year. But she knew her. If an uncle or cousin asked why Mona wasn't at Christmas her mother would make up a sob story about how Mona was mean and refused to talk to her. She wouldn't tell them the truth that Mona had called her mother from the hospital, asking her to please bring her a few things because she was in a locked ward.

"I just can't right now, Mona. You can't expect me to put my life on hold just because you're having a bad day."

"Mom, I have no one else to call. Mark won't take my calls. Please I just need a change of clothes. You live ten minutes from the hospital."

"I can't just drop everything, Mona. You can't just call and tell me what to do." Mona was biting her tongue, but then she heard her mother's boyfriend in the background telling her to bring him another beer.

"Just fucking forget it, *MOTHER*." Mona screamed. Her mother tried to say something but Mona slammed down the phone. The nurse at the station jumped. That was the last time she'd spoken with her. Now the whole family thought she was a crazy bitch. Only capable of taking care of ailing Gran.

But now Gran was dead, they all descended like Raven's eager to pick the leavings from dead Gran's remains. The house, the cars, the savings, any possessions worth anything. Mona already felt her head throbbing. She wanted to go back home and crawl into her casket with Frank. She'd had Gran put into a new coffin, one better suited to a petite little old woman.

The relatives were already bickering about who would get what before the dirt was dumped on Gran's bones. Mona heard whispers of "well she can't stay in that house all alone..." and "I don't think she had a will...No of course she's not getting everything. Why should she?"

Mona refused to host the family after the service was done. They ended up piling into their cars and driving off to an overpriced chain restaurant near the freeway. "You're welcome to join us." Aunt Susan said, opening the door to the Lincoln town car.

"I just buried my grandmother. I'm not very hungry." Mona told her and squeezed past two closely parked cars, heading for the gated exit. The afternoon was hot and the bugs whined over the slow tires rolling past. Mona felt them looking at her as she turned the corner and walked back towards the house.

It would be only a matter of time before they

came storming the house. Well they'd have to drag her. Where were they when Gran was living? When she needed help? She thought of all the times Gran would slap her or spit at her, try and wrestle away in a deep moment of blind confusion. Where was the family then? They took a depressed teenager and stuck her with her crazy grandmother and then left. They all left.

Mona locked the front door and walked through the house. The curtains were half open and half shut. Most of the lights had all been on for three days. Everything was almost the same as it was the morning that Gran died. Except for Frank Mona and placed him amongst the gentle soft folds of the casket.

God, that sounded good right now. She kicked off her sandals and pulled at her skirt and top. This was the first time all summer she had worn underwear. She hated it. Especially the panties. It didn't matter what cut she got, they were all uncomfortable and made more to highlight a woman's sex for a man, than for a woman's comfort. She kicked them off and threw them against her bedroom wall.

Frank looked up at her from the open lid. "It was horrible, Frank! You should have seen them all just staring down at her. Probably wondering if she was actually going to be buried with her diamond earrings." Mona shook her head and unhooked her flimsy bra. Another thing made more for the male gaze than

a woman's tits. The lace was scratchy, the cut barely there. What was the point? She threw it off, letting it
land on Frank.

"You don't care what I wear, do you? Bra or no
bra? Doesn't fucking matter." She climbed in, the cold
velvet brushing over her sweaty skin. She turned on
her side and rubbed her thumb in gentle whirls around
the temple of the skull.

She didn't know what she'd do without Frank.
The last few days she's told him everything about her
life, and he just listened. *Listened.* Didn't wait to speak.
Truly listened to her words instead of looking at her
chest. He didn't say he was going to call, then didn't.

In fact, Frank never said anything, and that
made Mona wetter than the humid air hanging outside
in the trees. Just his presence was enough, his flawless
touch when she rubbed him over her body. Light at
first. The glassy edges of teeth trailing over her nipples.

She liked being able to move him to where she
wanted him. A full body was heavy, she had to move
while he laid there. But Frank met her mouth with his.
He slid down her neck and over her tits, further until
he was burrowed deep between her thighs. Just where
she wanted him.

Mona got up from the coffin, on her knees.
Rubbed Frank between her legs, over her cunt. More
than a mere sex toy. He was more. A true lover. She

felt his transcended humanity lingering in the air as she gasped and fucked herself with his remains. She whined, and gasped, trembled and orgasmed, holding Frank clutched to her.

"Oh, *uh....*" She gasped feeling all the tension and sadness from the funeral seeping from her pores. Even her head felt light for a second. Then someone knocked at the door. Kept knocking. "Shit." Mona said.

She tossed Frank into the casket and slammed the lid. She pulled on her skirt, her blouse, and forgot about the rest of it. She was slick from Frank's head. Who knew a skull could be more patient, give better fucking head than a breathing man? She smirked at this. If more women knew how much pleasure the dead (or parts of the dead) could give them, she bet there would be a whole lot more female necros.

Men tended to think you just had to stick it in and the woman would orgasm against her will. If that was the case Mona would be seeking out corpses and risk potential criminal charges all for ten minutes of bliss, she couldn't even give herself. The first time she sat astride a corpse, she knew there would never be anything else to compare. The feeling of complete, utter acceptance. Wanting her. Her being the last before that body was forever entombed in the ground. A reverse virginity, Mona had named it.

Mona opened the front door, smoothing her

hair. "Yes?" Charles stood there. Nervous looking. He had a heavy blue dish in his hands.

"Mom wanted me to send this over. It's a casserole. Because…you know. Your grandmother and everything. She's not still here is she?" Charles asked, looking at Mona's haphazard appearance. The buttons were crooked, her skirt wrinkled.

"What? No. She's buried. The family is circling though. I thought it was one of them at the door, but I should have known better. They wouldn't bother knocking." Mona commented, wondering against what the hell was she going to do?

"Can I come in?" Charles asked, his hood hanging lower than normal.

"Why? I'm kinda busy." She pried the casserole from his fingers. "Just give it." She said. But he held on, ignoring her.

"I'll bring it in," he said walking past. She hated that he was bigger than her. He was looking around, walking towards the kitchen. Mona trailed behind, fiddling with buttons.

He stopped and walked backwards, peering into her room. The curtains were pulled shut, but a crack of light filtered in, reflecting off the dull surface of her box. "Shit, you really do have a coffin. I thought you were fucking with me." He set the casserole dish on the side table in the hallway.

"Charles? Stop." But Charles opened the casket, and found Frank sitting in his spot. The rage overcame him.

"Really, Mona? You've been fucking this skull the whole time? It's been what? Three or four days? And you've been fucking this?" He looked at the crusty bone that smirked up at him from ear to ear. He wanted to smash it between his hands. He regretted ever introducing her to Frank.

"This is why you won't sleep with me again? Because of him?!"

"Charles! My grandmother just died. We are not talking about this again. Why are you even here? You need to leave." Mona tried to sound firm. Like when she told Gran she had to wear shoes to go to the grocery store. Charles nodded like he couldn't believe it. Mona knew what he was going to do, but it all happened so fast. He picked up Frank and threw him against the far wall just over Mona's shoulder.

"Frank!" She screamed. Mona walked over and picked up Frank from the floor. He had a crack in his frontal lobe. She ran a finger over it, giving Charles an angry stare.

"You've got to be fucking kidding me! Mona? Just tell me...God, what's wrong with me that you'll blow me off to fuck a skull!? I'm sorry I'm not dead enough for you?!" He screamed. Mona stood still cradling Frank, shocked at the unfolding scene. She'd never heard Charles raise his voice. She had no idea Charles even cared if she slept with him again or not. It was only a few days ago.

Mona watched him rip off his red cloak. Underneath a plain black t-shirt and jeans. He was shoving his hand in his pocket. "How's this? Does this turn you on? Do you want me yet?" He flipped open a pocket knife and ran it down the center of his shirt, splitting the fabric. He threw it off.

"Charles, stop taking your clothes off. What are you doing?" She asked, feeling more confused than ever. Charles kicked his pants off and climbed into the casket. "Get out of there. *Charles*!" Her and Frank watched Charles laying in the casket, still, nude, and suddenly silent. Mona felt overwhelmed. She remembered another reason why she loved dead guys. They never pulled weird shit like this.

She set Frank on the dresser out of reach of Charles. She swallowed her annoyance. She was tired, worried about her future. She didn't want to deal with a naked man having a manic episode right now. It would help if she knew what was wrong with him. Was he having a bad day? In love with her? Or clinically insane?

She walked to the casket, looked down at him. "Charles?" She said, her voice soft, gentle, so as not to startle him to another fit. "Please open your eyes and look at me." His eyes fluttered and opened. He rolled them to the side, looking at her, but otherwise not moving. "You need to get up and put your clothes back on."

"Don't talk to me like I'm crazy, Mona. I'm not fucking crazy," he said, his words empty and far off. He sounded more like he was reflecting to himself, than talking to her. He was reminding himself he wasn't crazy.

"I know you're not. We all have our moments. But let's put your clothes on, okay?" They looked at each other in silence.

"Where's Frank?"

"I put him over there. Don't worry about him." She crouched down, chin resting on the side of the open casket. "Come on. I sleep in there, you know." She waited, he didn't flinch, kept staring up at her yellowed ceiling. "Charles. Charles. Charles..." She started to run on. He finally sighed and sat up, as if realizing his nonviolent protest was going nowhere. He could never compete with Frank.

Charles looked at Mona, "I jerked off thinking about you this morning, you know. And last night." he didn't seem embarrassed, but watched her to see what she would do. Mona's natural reaction was to flinch and look away, her cheeks burning with embarrassment.

"Charles, let's not talk about that. Come out here and let's put your pants on. Maybe we can get a drink or something. I hid a bottle of vodka in the back of the freezer." he nodded, accepting the fact she didn't care that he masturbated to her image. If a girl told him she touched herself thinking about him, he'd be flattered.

Mona was handing him his pants, she looked disheveled, tired, annoyed, but not flattered. He thought for sure the funeral would make her horny as well. Death did that to people. Apparently not a grandmother's death though. He admitted it himself, he'd miscalculated this one.

Charles pulled his pants back on, shoved his pocket knife back in his pocket. Didn't bother with the ripped open shirt. Shrugged his velvet crimson cloak on, pulled up the hood. Mona handed him the shirt. "No keep it," he said.

"Whatever." Mona walked out, stopped when she didn't hear Charles behind her. "Don't even think about it" She said, seeing him standing there glaring at Frank. "This has nothing to do with him. You're just not my type. There's nothing you can do about it."

Charles left the room and trailed down the hall behind Mona. He thought there was something he could do about it, but he wasn't sure if it was the right solution. He'd have to think about it for a day or two. He yanked out a chair at the table and dropped into it. His cape fluttered around him like a gown.

The frosted bottle hit against the glasses as Mona poured. She set one down before Charles. He looked at it but didn't drink. "I don't drink," he said.

"I see you drinking in your yard all the time. What are you talking about?" Mona asked, sipping. The cold dry bite rolled down her throat, like drinking rubbing alcohol only more rewarding. She took another drink.

"I quit." He shrugged and pushed the glass towards her. She dumped it into hers.

"When?"

"Just now. Frank doesn't drink either, does he?"

Mona slammed the glass on the table. "Christ, Charles! Really. Forget about Frank! He's just a skull."

"Just a skull? How many times have you fucked him since you brought him home?"

"That's none of your business." Mona said, hastily draining half the glass.

"He smells like cunt. You should wash him." Charles' words were dry and blunt.

"Alright you need to leave. You want to be an asshole and be jealous over a skull? I don't want to fuck you because you're not my type and I don't believe in using people."

"But I would be if I were-"

"Charles, stop! Just go." Mona shoved herself away from the table. She jerked open the back door, the late day sun creating a hot patch on the tile. "Charles!" She screamed. It had been a horrible day.

"Fine. Fine." he stopped in front of her, half out the door. "Have fun fucking *Frank*." He walked off, cloak blowing out behind him.

"Fuck you, Charles!" Mona yelled and slammed the door. She rubbed her forehead, walked back over to the table and drank from the vodka bottle. It was slippery, she dropped it, and it shattered around her feet. "Damn it." She moaned, cutting her foot while trying to creep around the mess for a towel. "Damn it. Damn it!"

Mona felt her world was cracking all around her. Gran was dead. She didn't know what would happen if she couldn't continue living in the house. She had no money. She wasn't even qualified to be a waitress. The whole thing worried her, she knew the family would come. They'd probably send Aunt Susan with a lawyer. Mona couldn't even afford her own lawyer.

The stress of worry created a sharp stabbing pain along the back of her neck. Similar to the fear she felt when forced to drive on the freeway. Her entire body was tense. Then this thing with Charles. She didn't know what was going on with him. She'd never seen anyone rip off their clothes like that, not even in the hospital. She wondered if he was on medication but was skipping it.

She walked back into her bedroom. She looked at the casket. Saw the ass print from where Charles had been. The nerve of that guy jumping into her bed. He thought what? Just because he was naked she was going to fuck him? She turned to Frank and lifted him from the dresser. He'd never think that.

"Frank," she said. Her tongue ran over the delicate spider webbed crack on his dented skull. It made her feel better. As if no matter where she might end up, she'd have Frank. Her silent, eternal, consort. She bet Frank never stripped off his clothes and climbed into a woman's bed hoping to seduce her.

Her mind went back to Charles feeling she made a big mistake fucking him. She didn't think he liked her that much, that he would even care. She'd seen him sitting in his lawn chair staring at the house, but she figured he was just looking off into space, not really focused on the house. The house just happened to be in his life of vision. Now she wasn't so sure. He had asked her out a handful of times, but he never sounded serious. Mona wasn't feeling she didn't know Charles as well as she thought she did.

Mona threw off her binding clothes and laid down in the soft velvet of her casket. Frank placed it between her breasts. "I think we just need to sleep,

Frank. We'll figure out what to do about Charles, and the house, *and* the family tomorrow." Mona said. It was still early, the low sun filtered through most of the windows.

Mona had already forgotten the habit of pulling the shades and turning on the lights in an attempt to keep the dark out. Gran was gone, there was no point. There was always a crack, and something would always get in, be it light or dark. Nothing could live in a vacuum.

Mona waited, tensed for days, expecting Aunt Susan. But Aunt Susan didn't show. Each time she heard a car roll by, she ran to the front window to look if it pulled in the driveway. Charles knocked at the back door. He peered through the windows. Mona sat crouched in the hall, or hiding behind the sofa avoiding him.

"Mona, please. I know you're in there. Just talk to me. Mona!" He shouted at the house. Later she'd slowly peek her head up over the window ledge and spot him sitting in the backyard smoking, looking determined. As if she was his girlfriend and he was going to win her back. There was no fucking way Mona was ever going to sleep with him again.

Frank spent the nights deep up in Mona's cunt, making love to her. It was the only thing that released her tension. It was just the two of them. Mona would place him on the velvet and straddle him, careful not to put too much weight on him, for fear of further aggravating the crack. Grinding, rubbing, she'd grip the sides of her casket, and just forget about everything else. She spent most of the day masturbating with Frank.

When the doorbell rang, Mona was climaxing, letting herself be as loud as she wanted to be. The gasps and screams made the orgasm better. Got out more of the anxiety. "Fuck me...Frank. *Frank*!" She screamed, back arched, forgetting to be careful she brought herself down hard upon him. Frank grinned and took it, the hair crack traveling further south along the optical crescent. Frank asked for nothing in return except her absolute pleasure.

Mona heard the doorbell but it was a few seconds before she could pull herself away. She hadn't heard the splinting of bone, but saw the damage she had done. "Frank...I'm so sorry." She said, holding the skull up to examine it. She flicked off a mark of white mucus from his forehead. "How could I be so careless?"

The doorbell rang again. "Damn it, if that's Charles..." She set Frank back in the velvet nest, pulled the lids closed. She'd have to find some super glue for Frank's injury. She didn't like the way it was starting to thread itself along the more delicate areas. She'd feel bad if she crushed in his eye socket with her sex. If he split in half she didn't know what she'd do. Those sharp ragged edges of bone ripping up her cunt wasn't her idea of a good time. And by now she was sure she wouldn't be able to replace him. They had been through too much in the past week.

Again with the doorbell. She wrapped herself in Gran's faded yellow robe and tied it shut. "Coming!" She said hurtling through the dim house to the front door. She should have looked, but didn't. On the porch stood Aunt Susan. "Mona, dear?" She asked, looking somewhat baffled by Mona's state of dress. "Is that Gran's bathrobe?"

Mona had the sudden urge to slam the door shut and pretend she wasn't home. But knew it would do no good. This was happening. "What, uh, can I do for you Aunt Sue?" She asked, pulling the robe tighter around her, folding her arms, to suggest Susan would not be coming in. Mona had a fear of letting the family in, they locked her out, and that would be that.

"Well I'm glad I caught you at home. We really need to talk, sweetie." She smiled, but it was tight and forced, as if trying to soften the blow of what was to come.

"The house is mine, Aunt Sue. Where has everyone been for the last two years? I mean come on." Mona just felt herself losing it, crashing towards hysteria. "I was just out of the hospital, for suicide! For a second time! And everyone thought it would be a good idea to make *me* Gran's primary caregiver? Then where did everyone go? Huh? I was nineteen. No, I think I'm owed this. Gran would want me to live here." Mona said.

Her words knocked Aunt Susan off her pedestal. She thought this would be easy. The family talked about maybe moving Mona into a small apartment until she got on her feet. "Well Mona, I'm surprised, frankly, you'd want to stay in this big old house by yourself. I mean, really? How could you even afford to keep it?" She laughed a little, her eyes darting back and forth.

"Well now that I have all this free time so maybe I can get a *paying* job, go back to school. Something. Don't worry about it. If I can take care of Gran I think I'll manage."

Aunt Susan thought to try a different approach, her face softened. "Mona, sweetie, come on now. Look at yourself. You're in your deceased grandmother's bathrobe in the middle of the day. You've never had a job before. This house is worth more being sold than living in it. It's practically falling down."

Mona snuffed at this. "I'm fucking staying, Sue. Get over it." She went to close the door, but Aunt Susan put up a hand to stop her.

"You can think whatever you want, Mona. Here take this," She handed Mona a small white card with a name and address. "I have an appointment with a lawyer tomorrow to go over Gran's will. We'll see what that has to say. I think you should make it a point to get dressed and be there." Her caring voice was cold and harsh. Mona ripped the card from her hands, gave a sharp smile and slammed the door, locking it.

"Bitch," she sighed and looked at the card. Yeah, she would be there.

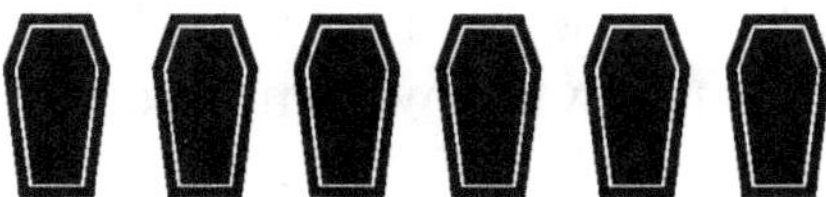

That evening Mona was walking around her room getting ready for bed. She was talking to Frank, going over the plan for the lawyer's office tomorrow. She had gathered all the papers she could find in the study. Records, whatever that would show how she had been Gran's primary caregiver for the last two years. That she was entitled to stay in the house.

She kept hearing scratching. Light at first, then rapid knocking on glass. She walked to the window and peered out into the encroaching dark. She jumped back when Charles appeared on the other side. "Mona," he said through the glass, his fingers drumming on the windowpane.

"Charles! What the hell are you doing?" She screamed, feeling completely exposed. What was he doing outside her window? Had he done this before? She recalled several times hearing things rustling in the bushes outside, but she always ignored it, thinking it was an animal. Now she was beginning to wonder.

She slid the window open. "Hey, what are you doing?" He asked casually, as if he weren't just hanging out, outside her bedroom window.

"I'm getting ready to go to sleep, Charles. I really don't have time for this. I have to go talk to a lawyer tomorrow, and I'm really kinda scared about it."

"Oh, that's too bad. I'm sure it'll be alright. Want to talk about it? I could come in if you want." He started to crawl through the window. Mona stopped him.

"No, Charles. I told you. We're not sleeping together again. We shouldn't have before, either. I don't know what I was thinking."

His face seemed to melt a little around the edges. "Don't even mention Frank." She said quickly knowing that's what he was thinking.

"Mona please. I think about you all the time. I just think-"

"Charles just stop it! Please listen. I don't want

to date you. I don't want to sleep with you. You need to go home. Just forget about it." She said, exhausted. She knew she sounded harsh, but he just wasn't listening.

He backed up from the window, as if she had just relieved a devastating revelation to him. "Mona...I..." he didn't finish but turned and fled into the night. Mona stood there a second to see if he'd come back. When she was satisfied he'd gone home she slid the window closed and locked it. Sighed.

"Fuck, Frank. Maybe we should sell the house." She really had no idea Charles even gave her a second thought. She undressed and climbed into the casket. Laid her head beside Frank's and looked up at the lid of her casket. She hadn't bothered to replace the photos. Gently, fingers traced bumps and the smooth surface of Frank. They had each other now, she didn't need anyone else.

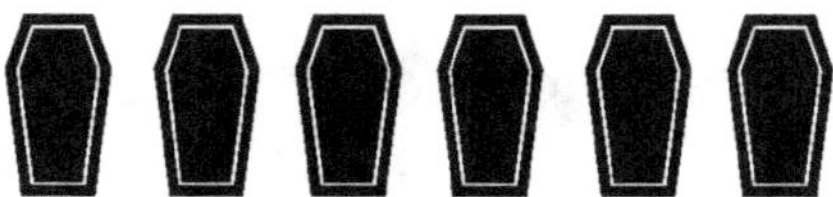

Mona dressed in a conservation blue skirt and black top. She pulled her hair back. She wore little make-up. She wanted to look responsible, but tired. As if taking care of Gran and her own mental health was draining every last drop of life from her bones, and to lose the house would be the final straw.

"Frank, what do you think? I think it looks

okay," she said. She didn't want to look too obvious. Frank gaped at her from the dresser. "You're right. Maybe I should keep my hair down." She pulled out the elastic band and let it sit on her shoulders. She looked at the clock. Saw she was running late.

She wanted to bring Frank along for moral support, but didn't feel like explaining herself. It wasn't *her* who robbed the tomb, but her one night stand. She set Frank in the casket. "I'll bring home some glue for the crack." She said, seeing it was growing deeper. Frank would have to start being on top from now on.

"I'll leave the lid open." She said, giving him one last look. He looked so beautiful and peaceful sitting there on the dark velvet, bathing in a cast of gentle early afternoon sun. Mona felt a reassurance settle over her, it would be alright. She would hold it together, and it would all work out. Wherever she ended up, she knew Frank would be there. He would be there to support her. That's what she needed most of all, someone who loved her unconditionally and wouldn't harp at her for making poor life choices. Who would threaten to leave because she was a little unconventional.

Charles heard Mona's garage door open next door. It was loud, and the old steel whined when the door opened, and then slammed shut afterward. He stood in his second story window, watching her pull out and drive off down the road. She must be going to talk to that lawyer, he figured. She'd be gone for a few hours at least. He'd made up his mind. He was giving himself to Mona. The only woman who would ever understand him. He was giving himself up as a personal tribute to her. If she wouldn't have him in life, he figured. Then death it was.

He felt the weight of the knife in his pocket. Without a moment of apprehension he left his room, not bothering to look back. His mother heard the rustle of his cloak coming down the stairs. She yelled something from the kitchen, he ignored her. Went to the back door, it was still jammed. Cursing silently to himself he walked back through the house. Went out the front door.

"Close the door!" His mother yelled behind him. Charles kept walking, heading for Mona's. He walked around back, tried the door to the kitchen. It opened and he went in without resistance. Instead it was still, as he expected. He wasn't interested in doing anything but what he came here to do.

The air conditioner hummed. The heavy velvet of his clock dragged over the carpet in the hallway. He stood in the doorway of Mona's room. Frank stared back from his place on the pillow inside the open casket. "Frank," Charles muttered, looking at the smug skull. Frank looked back, uncaring.

Charles walked over and picked him up. Moved

him back and forth in his hands. "What should I do with you?" Charles went over his options. He could take Frank back to the crypt. He could smash him. Toss him out in the road and hope he was run over. But that felt too good for Frank, the asshole who stole Mona's heart.

Charles knew he didn't have a lot of time. But he would get it done quickly and be done with it. "Fuck you, Frank!" He said, opening his cloak and shoving his trousers down to his ankles. He shoved his cock in Frank's cracked empty eye socket. "Fuck you. Fuck you," he said again and again thrusting into the cold, hard bone. "That's right, you're going to fucking take it. Just like you take everything!" Charles muttered, watching himself penetrate the empty orbital socket. He bent over, holding himself up on the bed, finishing inside Frank.

Frank didn't make a noise, except for the gentle splintering of bone as Charles shoved into him with a few lingering thrusts. Charles was pleased to see the drizzle he left behind oozing from Frank onto the bed. "Asshole," he said, turning away.

He looked back at the casket, it was now or never. He knew Mona would never forgive him for molesting Frank... unless he did this for her. He dropped his cloak, feeling the weight on his shoulders lift. Pulled off his shirt. Stood naked in the middle of the room. This was how he wanted to go. The thought of it aroused him all over again.

As Charles lay in the dark on the bed of cold velvet he thought about Mona. She would want him after this. Want his bones again, and again. This idea made him happy. They would both get what they ultimately wanted-death.

Mona didn't get home until nearly six in the evening. The lawyer's office was slow. She stopped and picked up Chinese food on the way home. Gran's will was updated a month after Mona had moved in, just before Gran completely lost her mind. Everything was to be hers. The family was not pleased. But it was iron-clad.

In the driveway, she looked up at the house, excited for the first time in her life to have a home. She could come and go as she pleased. Do what and whoever she pleased within the walls. Tomorrow she was going to start looking for a job. Maybe she could get a job as the groundskeeper at the cemetery. Whoever was in charge now was doing a pitiful job. She also wanted to go clean up Frank's family crypt as well.

Then she looked next door at Charles' house. A split level. Neatly kept. His window was empty. She expected him to be standing there, looking down on her. But the space was empty. It filled her with relief, maybe he wasn't as obsessed as he seemed to be. He left so quickly last night, he had to have gotten the message. She wished they could just go back to smoking in the backyard and staring at the dead grass.

Maybe with time they could. Summer was nearing an end. Soon everything would be heavy with snow. By next year maybe Charles would have a girlfriend and forgotten about their tryst in the cemetery. About his jealousy of Frank and her. *Frank*. She wanted to just go inside, peel off her clothes and get into the casket with Frank.

She wanted Frank between her thighs, massaging her with his glassy teeth, and the small bump on the bridge of his nose. She wondered if someone punched him in life and it healed wrong. Or maybe he was born with imperfection.

Mona liked that in a man. Imperfections. Pins in the legs, or scars on the skin. When she read about a suicide in the paper, the thought of lying over his tragic body inflamed her as nothing else could. That's what drew her to Charles, but in the end he felt empty. She could ask him anything, and he held no mystery to her. But a corpse, she would never know his inner self, because it was empty. Only his earthly body remained. Frank was a mystery to her. That small bump on his nose. Now the crack in his skull. Beautiful imperfection.

The house felt different as Mona stepped inside. As if someone was there going through her things. The air held a weight. "Hello? Frank?" She called, knowing he wouldn't answer, but hoping if someone was there they'd be frightened off by the indication of a male in the house. She walked down the hall to set her dinner on the kitchen table, but stopped at the door of her room.

The casket was closed. ...But she left it open. Frank was sitting right there sunbathing when she left. "Frank?" She walked closer, setting the bag of Chinese food on the floor. Maybe the lid just fell closed, she rationed. She looked over her shoulder, no one was there.

She felt she was being stupid, of course no one was here. No one was hiding in her box. Why would they? What would be the point? She opened the casket lid, and fell back, seeing Charles. He'd bled out all over the crushed velvet upholstery.

"Charles? Charles?!" Mona cried taking in the strange sight of the naked bloody boy in her bed. She crawled up to the edge and looked down at him. Frank was sitting beside him, a blood smear and something else stuck to his face.

"Oh Frank, what happened?" Mona picked

up the bone and wiped him off with the sleeve of her blouse. She set him gently on the bed, and looked back at Charles. "What the hell did you do, you stupid idiot?" She said out loud. She felt for a pulse, his skin was lukewarm, but his heart no longer sang in his chest. He'd probably been gone an hour more or less.

Charles was naked, his arms bloody. The lining of her casket soaking wet. The smell was strong, fresh death. It wasn't something she'd experienced before. A fleeting humanity, and she wondered what Charles felt before he slipped away. Tired? Relief? Or was he in pain? She hoped not.

Mona looked him in the eyes, which were half way closed, as if he were dosing. His was skin smooth and soft without that sticky sheen of summer sweat. She sighed and touched him more. Down his neck her fingers explored, over his prominent collar bone and along his sternum. Strummed her hands sweetly over his ribs.

She felt Frank glaring at her. "Frank, just look at him. I've never... he's so new." Mona thought about his red life soaking her bed. How his cooling corpse would feel beneath her. She thought maybe she could give him in death, what she couldn't in life - love, affection. Wasn't that what he wanted as well? He had done this to himself. He wanted her to see. He could have done it at home in the bathtub. But he was here, nude.

Presenting himself to her in the only way Mona would ever truly accept.

Mona fumbled for the zipper on her skirt and slid it off. Unbuttoned her blouse, "Don't worry I didn't forget about you, my love." She removed from the bed and brought Frank down into the casket with her. She spread her legs over Charles. Placed Frank over his face. Mona gasped, what a photo it made. Her dead boy and the dry skull he had gifted her in life. The two intertwined with her.

She felt tears crop up along her eyelids. "Thank you, Charles." She said with sincere gratitude.

Frank slid off to the side of Charles' face and sat on the pillow beside him. Mona was riding Charles hard, the blood smearing along her legs. She held his slashed hands to her bare breasts. They were clammy to the touch. She said his name and not Frank's when she finally came out the other side sweating and gasping with excitement.

But when she got up to take a bath, eat her dinner, it was Frank she took with her. She closed the lid on Charles. Seeming to forget about him until bed. When she lifted the lid, he looked pale. The blood left in his body pooled to his back, deep violet blossoms. She climbed in nude, not wanting to stain any of her clothes. Mona curled next to him, pulling his heavy, gore soaked cloak around her. She held Frank to her breast between herself and Charles' remains. The blood was cold now, but Mona was on fire.

# About the author

Elizabeth Bedlam lives, writes, designs
from Michigan, USA

www.ingramcontent.com/pod-product-compliance
Lightning Source LLC
Chambersburg PA
CBHW052121150726

48002CB00006B/2442